The Extraordinary
Mr Qwerty

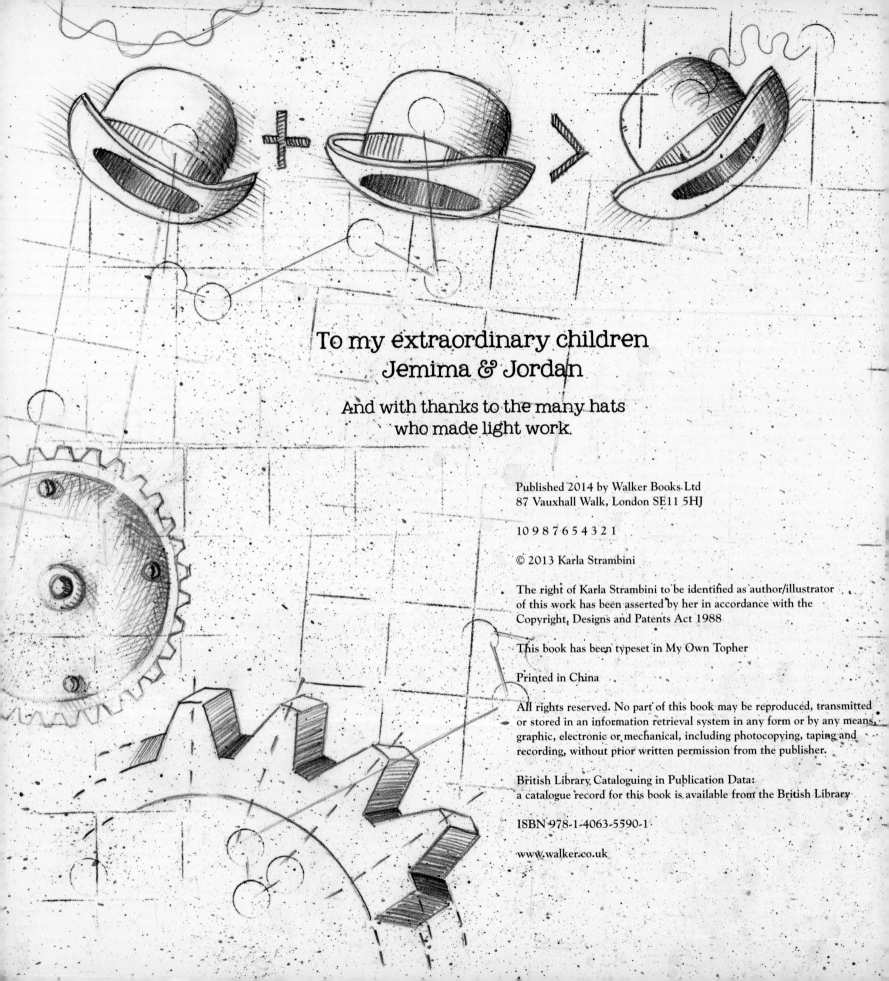

To my extraordinary children
Jemima & Jordan

And with thanks to the many hats
who made light work.

Published 2014 by Walker Books Ltd
87 Vauxhall Walk, London SE11 5HJ

10 9 8 7 6 5 4 3 2 1

© 2013 Karla Strambini

The right of Karla Strambini to be identified as author/illustrator
of this work has been asserted by her in accordance with the
Copyright, Designs and Patents Act 1988

This book has been typeset in My Own Topher

Printed in China

British Library Cataloguing in Publication Data:
a catalogue record for this book is available from the British Library

ISBN 978-1-4063-5590-1

www.walker.co.uk

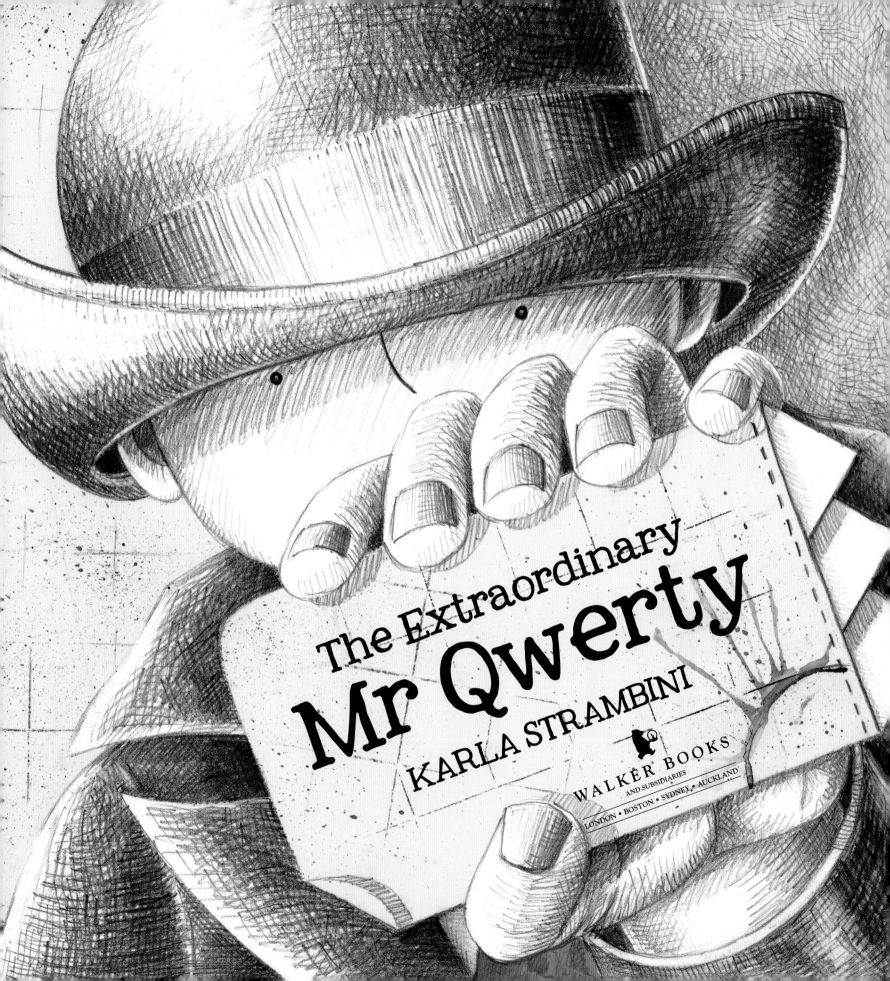

The Extraordinary
Mr Qwerty

KARLA STRAMBINI

WALKER BOOKS
AND SUBSIDIARIES
LONDON • BOSTON • SYDNEY • AUCKLAND

There once was a man

named Norman Qwerty

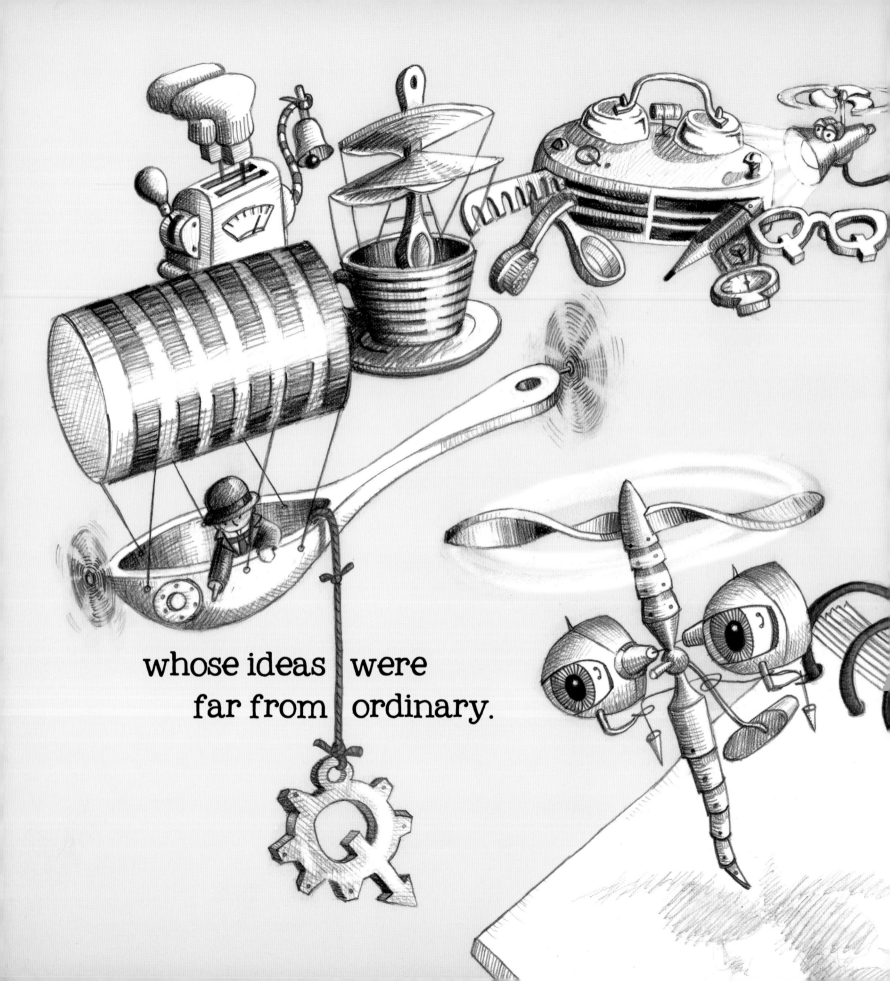

whose ideas were far from ordinary.

the way that Mr Qwerty thought

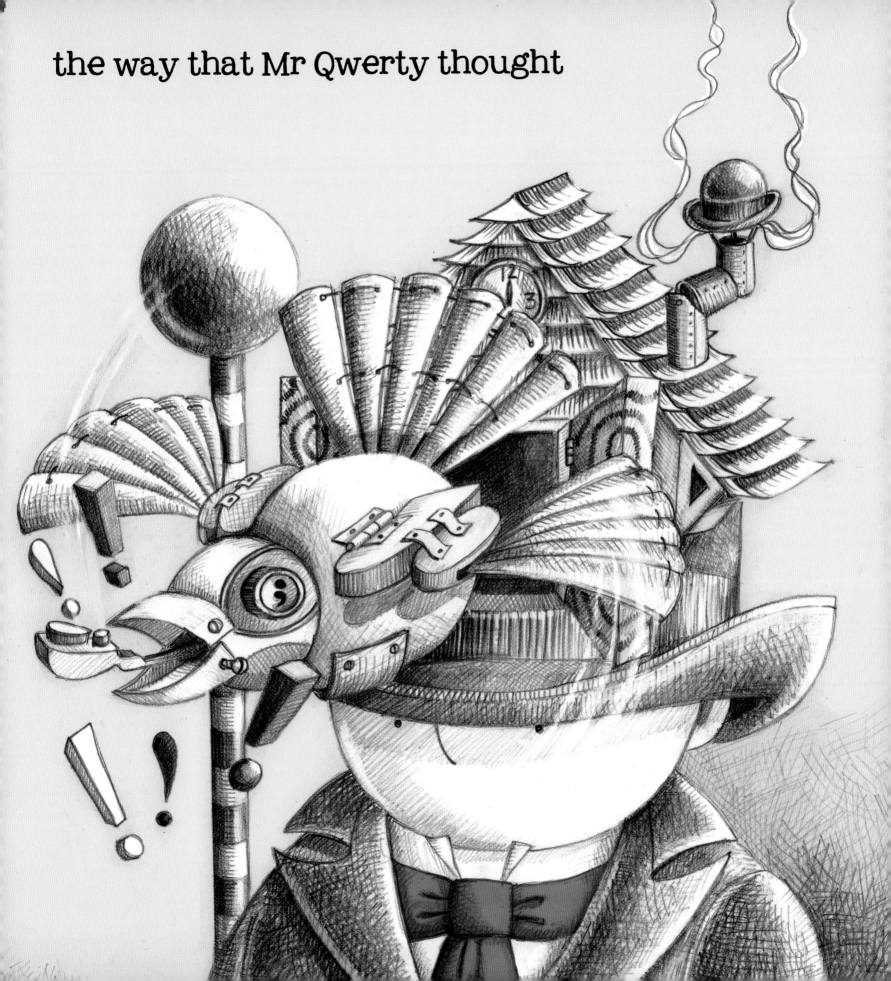

or so he thought.

Mr Qwerty was afraid
that people would think
his ideas were strange,

and he felt completely
alone.

...most of the time.

But when his ideas escaped,

as ideas often do,

they GREW,

and GREW,

until they were

SO BIG,

that something had to be done about them.

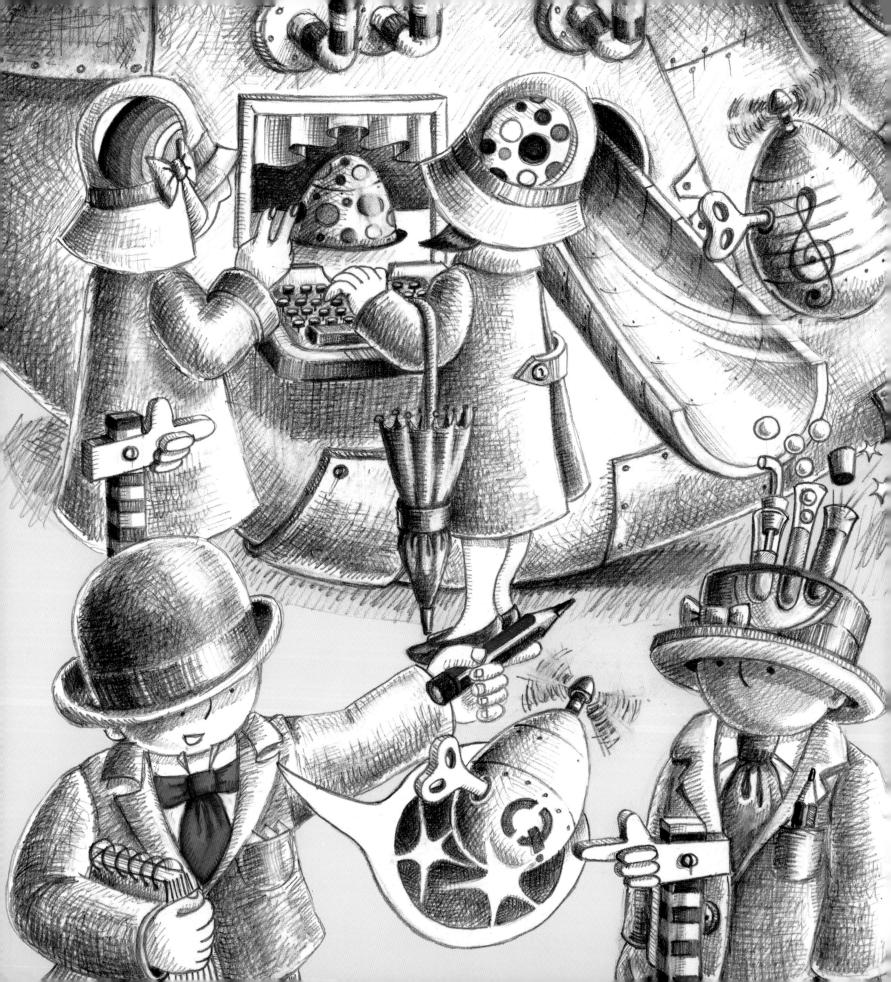

Mr Qwerty built
the most
EXTRAordinary
thing that anyone
had ever seen.

The world, from that moment forth,

was never quite the same

and Mr Qwerty
was never alone.